TREASURY OF

Phoenix International Publications, Inc.
7390 North Lincoln Avenue
Lincolnwood, Illinois 60712

Lower Ground Floor, 59 Gloucester Place
London W1U 8JJ

Permission is never granted for commercial purposes.

www.pikidsmedia.com

pi kids is a trademark of Phoenix International Publications, Inc.,
and is registered in the United States.

8 7 6 5 4 3 2 1

Manufactured in China.

ISBN: 978-1-4508-5445-0

TREASURY OF
Animal Tales

 phoenix international publications, inc.

Contents

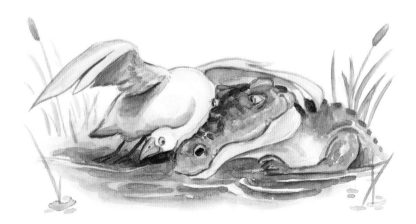

The Tortoise and the Hare

Adapted from Aesop's fable
Illustrated by Viviana Diaz Khalsi

In the woods there lived a very slow Tortoise and a very swift Hare. The Hare was a proud animal and well aware of his speedy talents. He took delight in taunting the humble Tortoise.

One morning, the Tortoise was plodding along when the Hare began to run circles around him.

"I just saw a snail slither by faster than you!" said the Hare.

"Perhaps you did," said the Tortoise. "I may be a slow creature, but I'd like to challenge you to a race."

"*You?* Challenge *me* to a race?" laughed the Hare.

The noisy laughter of the Hare caught the attention of the other animals. They liked the idea of watching a good race.

The next morning, the Tortoise slowly made his way to the starting line.

The Hare was still in bed. He had been up all night bragging to the other animals about his upcoming victory over the Tortoise.

Soon it was time for the race to begin. The Tortoise was ready. The Hare was just waking up.

"On your marks!" barked the Fox. "Get set!"

"Whoa! Don't start without me!" The Hare dashed to his place at the starting line.

"GO!" squeaked the Mouse.

"See you at the finish line!" laughed the Hare, leaving the Tortoise in a cloud of dust. The Hare ran so fast that he was out of sight in an instant.

When the dust settled at the starting line, the Tortoise had only taken a few steps.

"Ha, ha," laughed the Hare to himself as he raced far ahead of the Tortoise. "I'll show that old Tortoise! He should have known better than to think he could beat me in a race."

Soon the Hare grew tired. He had run so fast that he was halfway through the racecourse.

"I am far ahead of that Tortoise," thought the Hare. "I think I'll take a rest until he comes along. That ought to show him how foolish he is to race me!" Then he stretched out on a hammock.

The Hare found a few carrots and enjoyed a snack.

After he'd eaten his fill, he felt sleepy. "Well, I suppose there's no harm in taking a nap," the Hare said. He shut his eyes and soon he was sound asleep.

Meanwhile, the Tortoise was making slow but steady progress along the path.

The Tortoise happily moved along one step at a time, enjoying the scenery and greeting the other animals along the way. After quite some time, he came upon the sleeping Hare. The Tortoise tried to be quiet as he passed the foolish Hare. He noticed his friend Squirrel in a nearby tree.

"Hello, Squirrel," said the Tortoise. "It's a beautiful day, isn't it?"

"Yes," said Squirrel. "Keep up the good work!"

"Thank you," replied the Tortoise.

While the foolish Hare continued to sleep, the Tortoise patiently made his way down the trail, climbing hills and crossing forests. Hours passed as he crept past a brook, moseyed through a field, and walked beside a pond.

Next the Tortoise passed his friend Owl.

"Great job!" hooted Owl.

"Thank you," replied the Tortoise.

"I can see the finish line from here!" Owl cheered from up in a tree.

Soon the Tortoise could see the finish line in the distance. Still the Hare dozed away.

As the sun sank low in the sky, a cool breeze blew, chilling the Hare. At last, he awoke.

The Hare yawned and rolled out of the hammock. He noticed the sun was setting.

Then the Hare remembered the race.

"The Tortoise! I must get back to the race!"

"You better hurry if you want to win," said the Squirrel. "The Tortoise passed by hours ago."

"How could the Tortoise be winning? I'd better get moving!" The Hare darted off in a panic.

The Hare scampered along, tripping and falling as he scrambled to make up for lost time. The Hare went as fast as he could, and as he went over the last hill, he could see the Tortoise ahead of him, crossing the finish line.

"I declare, the Tortoise has beaten the Hare!" roared Bear.

As the animals cheered and congratulated the Tortoise, the Hare came puffing toward the finish line, completely out of breath.

"How did you beat me?" the Hare asked, catching his breath. "I'm so fast!"

"You *are* fast, Mr. Hare," said the Tortoise.

"And you're so slow!" huffed the Hare.

The Tortoise nodded. "I may be slow, but I am patient and steady, and I never stopped going. You see, my friend, slow and steady wins the race!"

The Tortoise celebrated his victory, and the story of how he outran the Hare has become a legend and a lesson for generations to come, teaching us that perseverance is an important virtue to have.

The Bear Went Over the Mountain

Illustrated by Lisa Alderson

The bear went over the mountain,
The bear went over the mountain,
The bear went over the mountain,
To see what he could see.

And all that he could see,
And all that he could see,
Was the other side of the mountain,
The other side of the mountain,
The other side of the mountain,
Was all that he could see.

The Elephant's Child

Adapted from the story by Rudyard Kipling
Illustrated by Jane Miles-Smith

 any years ago elephants did not have long trunks. They ate leaves from low branches. They had to get on their knees to drink water from pools.

One day a baby elephant was walking in the jungle and he saw a hippo.

"Why are you so fat?" the little elephant asked.

"Don't be
so rude!" snorted
the hippo.

Then he saw a leopard.

"Why do you have those spots?"

"*Grrr,*" growled the leopard.

"Mind your own business!"

Then the elephant saw a crocodile resting on the bank of a river.

"Hello," the little elephant said. "Are you a log?"

"Yes," said the crocodile, annoyed with the little elephant's question.

The little elephant was very curious. "What does a log eat with those big teeth?"

"Come closer and

I will tell you," the crocodile smiled.

The curious little elephant leaned in.

"I EAT BABY ELEPHANTS!" said the

crocodile, grabbing the little elephant's nose.

"Help!" cried the little elephant.

The crocodile pulled on the little

elephant's nose. The little elephant

pulled to get away.

They pulled so long and hard that the little elephant's nose grew longer and longer and longer.

Finally the crocodile let go of the little elephant and swam away. But now the little elephant's nose was very long. It almost touched the ground.

Now the little elephant didn't have to kneel to drink from the river. He liked that. And now he could squirt water over his back. He liked that, too.

The little elephant was hungry, but he did not have to eat the leaves on the ground. Now he could reach the best leaves that grew high in the trees!

Other elephants saw his long nose.

"We want long noses, too,"
the other elephants said.

"Go to the river, and look for
the log with sharp teeth," he said.

One by one, the other elephants
went to have their noses stretched. And
that's why elephants have long noses today!

Where Has My Little Dog Gone?

Illustrated by Jeremy Tugeau

Oh, where, oh, where has my little dog gone?
Oh, where, oh, where can he be?
With his ears cut short and his tail cut long,
Oh, where, oh, where can he be?

I'm Just a Little Puppy

Illustrated by Jeremy Tugeau

I'm just a little puppy and as good as can be,
And why they call me naughty I'm sure I cannot see.
I've only carried off one shoe and torn the baby's hat,
And chased the ducks and spilled the milk —
there's nothing bad in that!

How Brer Rabbit Outsmarted the Frogs

Adapted from the Southern folktale
Illustrated by James Hoston

Brer Raccoon loved to catch frogs. He caught so many that the frogs called a meeting. They were tired of being caught. The bullfrog said, "I will watch for that raccoon. If he comes along, I will warn you."

The next day, Brer Raccoon came home with an empty sack. This made his wife very angry.

Early the next morning, Brer Raccoon found his friend Brer Rabbit fishing down by the river.

"Howdy-do, Brer Raccoon," said the rabbit.

"See this bump on my head?" said Brer Raccoon. "My wife hit me with a broom. I can't seem to catch those wild frogs anymore."

"Well, I think you need a plan," said Brer Rabbit. "Next time you come to the river, fall down and play dead like Brer Possum. Just lie there and don't move till I tell you to."

"That is a mighty fine plan," said Brer Raccoon. "I don't understand it, but it sure sounds smart."

33

The next time Brer Raccoon went to the river, he heard the bullfrog call, "Here he comes!"

Brer Raccoon remembered the plan. He marched to the river and groaned, "I'm starving to death. I haven't had any frogs to eat for days."

Then he fell back like he was dead. The frogs popped their eyes above the water and watched.

Brer Rabbit came by and said, "I guess someone should dig him a grave. I'm so torn up with grief, I don't believe that I can."

"We can dig it! We can dig it!" said the frogs. They got their shovels and started to dig.

The frogs dug and dug. Brer Raccoon, who was still pretending to be dead, went down into the ground, and all the frogs went down with him.

Suddenly Brer Rabbit called down into the hole, "Brer Raccoon, pick up your supper. This pit is too deep for those frogs to jump out of."

So Brer Raccoon started grabbing frogs and throwing them into his sack.

All the frogs yelled, "He tricked us!"

Thanks to Brer Rabbit's plan, Brer Raccoon and his wife had enough to eat for that year and the next year, to boot! And that's the end of that.

There Was a Little Pig

There was a little pig,

Who wasn't very big,

So they put him in a great big show.

While playing in the band,

He broke his little hand,

And now he can't play his old banjo.

38

The Crocodile and the Goose

Illustrated by Aaron Boyd

t was a bright sunny morning on the banks of the great river. The forest was alive. Snake slithered out of his hole to lie in the sun. Bugs swarmed among the twisted branches.

Later that morning, Goose waddled out of her nest to peck and scratch for acorns and grain.

Crocodile loved to float like a log, listening to the sounds of the river. He loved the warmth of the sun on his scaly, green skin. And he loved looking for his next meal.

Crocodile saw Goose, but she didn't see him. "Mmmm," Crocodile said. "I'd love a nice, fat goose for breakfast."

The water carried Crocodile down the great river, closer and closer to Goose.

"Mmmm," said Goose. "This grain is delicious." She paused to shake her feathers in the warm sun.

Slowly, Crocodile paddled ashore. He watched Goose. "Mmmm," Crocodile said to himself. "That round, feathered belly sure looks delicious."

Goose stood on the river bank. Crocodile opened his mouth, ready to grab her.

"Hey, brother!" Goose cried. "You can't eat me!"

"Why?" Crocodile asked.

"I'm your sister, and you can't eat your family."

"Are we family?" Crocodile asked. He slinked back into the river and swam away, confused.

Crocodile was still hungry and thought all night about Goose. "That bird sure would taste good."

The next morning, Goose was sunning herself on the riverbank. Crocodile swam across the river and leaped out of the water, ready to grab Goose.

"Hey, brother!" shouted Goose as she flew away. "Eating family just isn't right."

Crocodile's empty stomach growled. The angry, hungry crocodile lay there and began to cry.

"What's wrong, Crocodile?" Snake asked.

"I want to eat Goose," said Crocodile, "but she said we are family. But she has feathers and a beak, while I have tough skin and sharp teeth."

"Sure," said Snake, "but Goose swims just like you. Crocodiles and geese both lay eggs. And you both hunt for food in the riverbank sand."

Crocodile finally had to agree. And that is why crocodiles, to this very day, never eat geese.

Gray Goose

Illustrated by Martin Irish

Gray goose and gander,

Waft your wings together,

And carry the king's daughter

Over the one-strand river.

Three Billy Goats Gruff

Adapted from the Norwegian fairy tale
Illustrated by Tim Ellis

Once there were three Billy Goats Gruff. The oldest was Big Billy Goat Gruff, who wore a thick collar of black leather. Next was Middle Billy Goat Gruff, who had a red collar around his medium-sized neck. Finally, there was Little Billy Goat Gruff, whose yellow collar was small and thin, just like him.

Big Billy Goat Gruff
had a deep billy goat
voice. Middle Billy Goat Gruff
had a middle-sized billy goat voice.
And Little Billy Goat Gruff had a tiny
squeak of a billy goat voice. All winter, the
three Billy Goats Gruff lived on a rocky hillside.

During the cold winter, the three Billy Goats
Gruff kept warm by playing among the rocks.
Big Billy Goat Gruff was the best climber
and the strongest. He had powerful legs and big,
curved horns. His brothers loved watching him
jump over the biggest, steepest rocks.

Middle Billy Goat Gruff
and Little Billy Goat Gruff cheered
as Big Billy Goat Gruff ran and jumped.

Next to their hill ran a powerful, rushing river. At night, the cold winter wind would blow up from the river and chill the three Billy Goats Gruff.

Little Billy Goat Gruff looked up to see the sky filled with bright, shining stars.

Middle Billy Goat Gruff looked up to see the thin sliver of the winter moon.

"Enough looking up at the sky," said Big Billy Goat Gruff. "It is time to find a place to sleep."

So the three Billy Goats Gruff found a cozy cave for the night. The cave kept them out of the cold, and the three Billy Goats Gruff grew sleepy.

Soon it was springtime. From their hillside, the three Billy Goats Gruff looked longingly across the rushing river to the green, grassy meadow beyond.

"How I would love to go to the meadow and eat that sweet grass," said Little Billy Goat Gruff. "The winter was long, and now I'm hungry."

"To get to the meadow," said Middle Billy Goat Gruff, "we have to cross the bridge over the river."

But the three Billy Goats Gruff knew that under the bridge lived a mean, ugly troll. The troll had eyes as big as saucers, a head of shaggy, greasy hair, and a nose that was as long as a broomstick.

The three Billy Goats Gruff also knew that the wicked troll said he would eat any billy goats that tried to cross his bridge. He was a nasty fellow.

"It isn't safe for you two to go across the bridge," said Big Billy Goat Gruff. "That troll will surely gobble you up. But I have a plan."

The next morning, the three Billy Goats Gruff went down to the river. Little Billy Goat Gruff started to cross the bridge.

Trip-trap, trip-trap, trip-trap, went Little Billy Goat Gruff's tiny hooves on the bridge.

"Who's that *trip-trapping* across my bridge?" roared the troll.

"It is only I, Little Billy Goat Gruff."

"I'm coming to gobble you up!" said the troll.

"Oh, no!" cried Little Billy Goat Gruff. "I am but a tiny billy goat. Wait for my brother. He will make a much bigger meal for you."

So the troll let Little Billy Goat Gruff cross the
bridge to the other side. Then that hungry troll
patiently waited for Middle Billy Goat Gruff to
come *Trip-Trapping* across the bridge.

In a little while, Middle Billy Goat Gruff started
across the nasty troll's wooden bridge.

Trip-Trap, Trip-Trap, Trip-Trap, went
Middle Billy Goat Gruff's medium-sized hooves.

"Who's that *Trip-Trapping* across my bridge?" roared the hungry old troll.

"It is only I, Middle Billy Goat Gruff," said the second billy goat.

"Well," said the troll, "I'm coming to eat you!"

"Oh, no!" said Middle Billy Goat Gruff in a medium-sized voice. "I'm but a middle-sized billy goat. If you were smart, you would wait for my brother, Big Billy Goat Gruff. He is ever so large and would make a much bigger dinner than me."

The hungry troll thought that was a good idea and let Middle Billy Goat Gruff cross the bridge.

61

Finally, Big Billy Goat Gruff walked onto the bridge. *TRIP-TRAP*, *TRIP-TRAP*, *TRIP-TRAP*, went his very large and very heavy hooves.

"Who's that *TRIP-TRAPPING* across my bridge?" roared the troll.

"It is I, Big Billy Goat Gruff," said the largest of the billy goat brothers.

"Well, here I come to eat you up!" said the troll.

The troll climbed onto the bridge and found
the largest, strongest billy goat he'd ever seen.

With his big horns, Big Billy Goat Gruff tossed
the troll off the bridge and into the river below.

The troll was gone, and the three Billy Goats Gruff were together again on the other side of the bridge where the grass was sweet and green.

So the three Billy Goats Gruff spent their summer eating and playing in the meadow. Best of all, they knew they were safe, as that nasty old troll was never seen again.

Bell Horses

Illustrated by Jeremy Tugeau

Bell horses, bell horses,
What time of day?
One o'clock, two o'clock,
Three and away.

The Wise Old Owl

Illustrated by Jeremy Tugeau

A wise old owl sat in an oak.
The more he heard, the less he spoke;
The less he spoke, the more he heard.
Why aren't we all like that wise old bird?

Four Friends

Illustrated by Cathy Johnson

at, Bird, Snake, and Turtle were best friends until they had a fight one day.

"I hear that in the city the houses are as tall as mountains," said short-legged Turtle.

"No, the houses are little boxes," said Bird.

"Maybe some are like mountains and some are like boxes," said Cat.

"Or mountains that *are* boxes," said Snake.

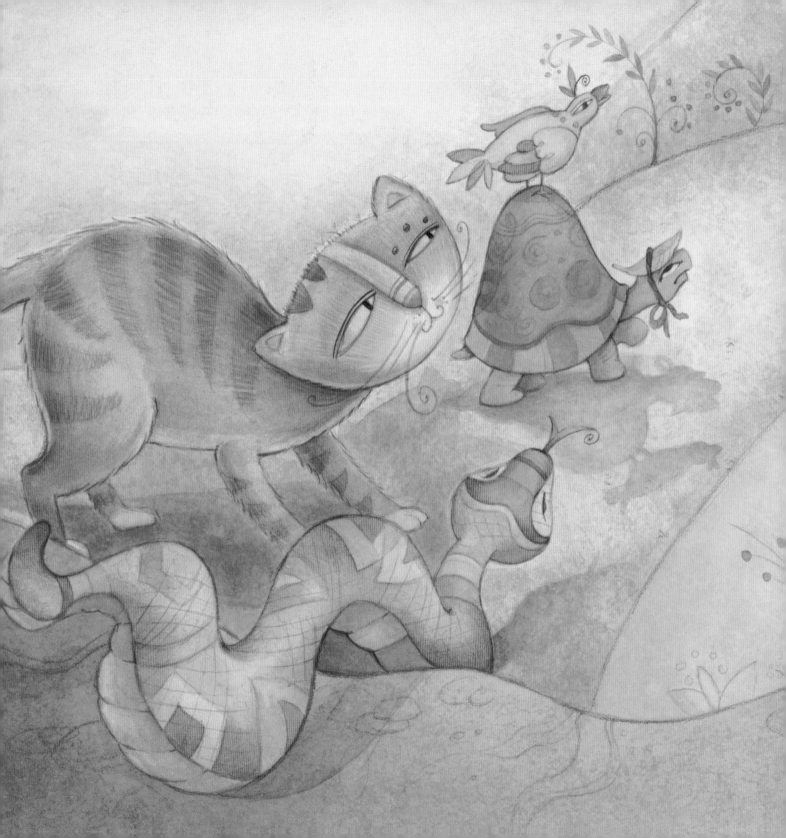

The four friends argued until the next day, when they began the long journey to the city to see for themselves. They walked and argued for days. "Mountains!" "Boxes!" "Mountains!" "Boxes!"

"I've got to go back," said Cat one day. "I cannot find my water bowl."

"We'll go on," said the others. "You catch up."

Several days later, they passed a palm-nut tree. "I'm hungry," said Bird. "I want some nuts."

"It will be a long time before those nuts are ripe," said Turtle and Snake. But Bird decided to stay until the nuts were ready to eat.

After many days, Snake and Turtle came to a branch that lay across the road. Snake slithered right over it, but Turtle's legs were too short.

"I don't want to leave you," Snake said, "but I want to see the city." So Snake left Turtle behind.

Snake grew hungry and decided to eat. His friends would have warned him that snakes cannot move for a long time after a meal. But soon Snake had a full belly, and could only lie on the road.

By then, Cat had found his water bowl. Bird had eaten the palm nuts. Turtle had finally gotten past the tree branch. And Snake began to move.

As Snake crawled, he looked up and saw Bird. She swooped down and carried Snake in her beak. The two friends were so happy to see each other that they forgot to argue. After a short while, they saw Cat, with Turtle riding on her back.

The four friends finally made it to the city. They saw that the houses were neither as tall as mountains or as small as little boxes.

"Oh, no!" said Cat. "We were all wrong."

"Maybe so," said Turtle, "but we found something very important..."

"Yes," said Bird. "We found each other!"

The Horse and the Flea

Illustrated by Susan Spellman

A horse and a flea and three blind mice

Met each other while skating on ice.

The horse, he slipped and fell on the flea.

The flea said, "Oops, there's a horse on me!"

The Ant and the Grasshopper

Adapted from Aesop's fable
Illustrated by Jason Wolff

Summer had just begun. Animals and insects scurried about.

"Summer's here! The best time of the year!" the Grasshopper sang.

An ant marched past the Grasshopper, carrying small seeds and bits of food.

"What are you doing?" asked the Grasshopper.

"Summertime is for planning and gathering for the winter," said the Ant.

"Winter is far away. I think I'd rather go and play," sang the Grasshopper. With that, the Grasshopper hopped off into the cornfield.

The Grasshopper forgot about the Ant and leaped onto a cornstalk. A soft leaf gave him a bed. Above him, another leaf gave him shade. And within reach, smaller, tender leaves gave him food.

All summer, the Grasshopper watched the ants gather food. Then one day, the Grasshopper heard a strange noise in the cornfield.

The farmer was coming to harvest the corn! The Grasshopper jumped into the grass. "Close call, all in all," sang the Grasshopper. "I just lost my bed and food!"

The Ant was marching past and heard the Grasshopper. "There's still time for you to store food and find shelter," the Ant said

"Not today!" the Grasshopper said. He hopped to a toadstool and fell asleep. Suddenly, an acorn fell from a tree and knocked his toadstool over.

"I'm sorry," chattered a squirrel above him. "My paws were so full that I dropped some acorns."

The Grasshopper hopped off to the apple orchard. He was just settling down when the ants began marching by again, carrying apples that had fallen from the trees.

"You again!" the Grasshopper said to the Ant. "I thought by now you'd have enough. You can't eat all that stuff!"

The Ant smiled, but he did not stop to talk. "It's always better to have a little extra than not enough," he called.

The Grasshopper frowned. The sun was setting, and it was starting to get cold.

The Grasshopper shivered. He looked around for a sunny spot, but the sun was gone from the sky. The sun was one thing the Grasshopper didn't mind seeing at work. With each day, though, it seemed to work less and less.

One day, the Grasshopper felt especially cold. "I think I'll visit my friends, the mice. They are always nice!" he sang.

The Grasshopper crept into the home of the field mouse family. It was warm inside, but very crowded. So crowded that there wasn't enough room for him to stay.

The Grasshopper hopped back to the orchard. The ground was so cold now that it hurt his feet.

Suddenly snow began to fall. It covered the Grasshopper. With a jump, he fluttered his wings. He had to get inside or he would freeze! Hopping as fast as he could, the Grasshopper raced to the Ant's house.

"Is anybody home?" he called into the tunnels.

"Why aren't you playing in the snow?" asked the Ant.

The Grasshopper explained he had just come by for a visit. But he shivered and looked cold.

The Ant felt bad, but wanted to be sure that the Grasshopper understood the value of hard work. "We got our food for the winter by working hard. If you stay with us this winter, you'll have to work hard, too."

The Grasshopper agreed.

"Your job will be to sing for us!" the Ant said.

That winter, the Grasshopper sang for the Ant and his huge family. And the next summer, the Grasshopper helped to gather food, singing, "Summer work is slow and steady. But come winter, I'll be ready!"

Five Little Monkeys

Illustrated by Katherine Kirkland

Five little monkeys jumping on the bed,
One fell off and bumped his head.
Mama called the doctor and the doctor said,
"No more monkeys jumping on the bed!"

Why Frog and Snake Never Play Together

Adapted from the African folktale
Illustrated by Aaron Boyd

One sunny afternoon Snake and Frog were going along their way, when they almost bumped into each other.

Frog asked Snake, "What are you?"

"I'm a snake. I slither," Snake said. "What kind of snake are you?" she asked Frog.

Frog laughed. "I'm not a snake, I'm a frog!"

As Frog and Snake wandered together into the bush, they decided to become friends.

Frog and Snake snacked on fruit flies and crunchy bugs. Frog showed Snake how to hop. "Watch me!" she said as she hopped up, up in the air and came down with a *PLOP!* Snake showed Frog how to slither. She went to the top of a mound and slid down — *SWOOSH!*

Dusk arrived and they knew it was time to go home. They agreed to play the next day.

When Frog came home, her mother was surprised to see her covered with grass.

"What happened?" she asked.

Frog replied, "I was playing with a snake!"

Ma Frog was horrified. "Dear child, don't you know that snakes eat frogs? You must promise me that you will never play with snakes again."

Nearby, Snake arrived home. Ma Snake said, "My, my. You look tired. Where have you been?"

Snake happily replied, "I have a new friend named Frog. We played together."

Ma Snake was shocked, "A frog? You're a snake, and snakes are supposed to eat frogs! The next time you see her, you must gobble her up."

The next day Snake went to Frog's house and called out, "Frog, let's play together!"

Frog huddled inside her house. "Ha!" she said. "My mother told me how snakes really play."

"My mother talked to me, too," Snake said. "She told me all about frogs and what I'm supposed to do." Snake didn't know what else to say.

"I guess this is good-bye," Frog said.

"Good-bye," Snake said as she sadly slithered away.

Frog and Snake never played with each other again. However, they always wondered if things could have been different. If you look carefully, you might see them sitting very quietly in the sun remembering their day.

The Little Mouse

Illustrated by Marnie Webster

I have seen you, little mouse,

Running all about the house,

Through the hole your little eye

In the wainscot peeping sly,

Hoping soon some crumbs to steal,

To make quite a hearty meal.

Look before you venture out,

See if kitty is about.

The City Mouse & the Country Mouse

Adapted from Aesop's fable
Illustrated by Dominic Catalano

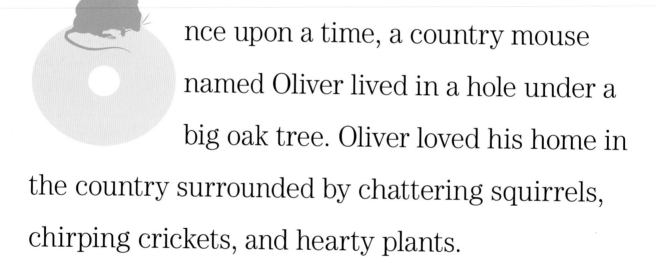

nce upon a time, a country mouse named Oliver lived in a hole under a big oak tree. Oliver loved his home in the country surrounded by chattering squirrels, chirping crickets, and hearty plants.

One day Oliver decided to invite his city cousin, Alistair, for a visit.

"Alistair will surely like it here," Oliver thought.

When Alistair arrived, he set his fine leather suitcase on Oliver's rug of fresh pine needles.

"Oliver, is this your cellar?" he asked.

"No, it's my home," said Oliver. He and Alistair sat down for dinner and ate barley, wheat, and dandelion tea.

Alistair nibbled his meal politely. "This tastes as though it's good for me, although it doesn't have much flavor!" he chuckled to himself.

After dinner they both settled into their beds and went to sleep.

The next morning, a robin family twittered in the oak tree.

"I love the sound of birds in the morning," said Oliver. "It makes me excited to start my day."

"You start your day this early?" asked Alistair. "I can't stand that confounded racket!" Alistair pressed his pillow to his ears.

Oliver put on his overalls, pulled up his work boots, and pushed his wheelbarrow out into the sunshine to begin his day. Alistair yawned and rolled out of bed. He thought it was too early and too hot to do any work.

CITY

Alistair watched his cousin collect acorns, corn husks, and water. After Oliver finished, Alistair said "I think it's high time for a snack and a nap."

Oliver giggled. "My work isn't finished."

Alistair sighed. "You work too hard for your dinner here, and all you end up with is a pile of seeds! Come back to the city with me, and I'll show you the good life."

So the two mice set out for Alistair's home in the city. Oliver followed Alistair over fields and valleys, into subway tunnels, and across crowded city parks until they arrived on Alistair's street.

Alistair stopped in front of a beautiful hotel.

"Welcome to my home! This is how mice should really live," he said.

Oliver stared up at the revolving glass door. "But how do we get in?" he asked.

"We wait until it turns, and then we run through as fast as we can!" said Alistair.

When the door started to turn, Alistair darted inside. Oliver tried to keep up with his cousin, but his bag became caught in the door. Oliver went round and round so many times, he couldn't tell whether he was right side up or upside down!

Finally, Alistair pulled Oliver out of the door, and led him across a beautiful marble hallway to a small crack hidden by heavy velvet drapes. "Here is my apartment!" Alistair announced.

Oliver looked around in amazement. There were so many fancy things everywhere!

"We're under the bandstand," Alistair told Oliver. "An orchestra plays at night and people dance till morning."

"Isn't it too loud to sleep?" asked Oliver.

"Sleep?" asked Alistair. "I sleep when I want! I never have to worry about being up early."

Alistair led Oliver into the chef's kitchen. "You don't want anyone to catch you," he warned.

Oliver was nervous. What would happen to them if they were caught?

Alistair quietly opened the pantry door. Inside Oliver saw shelf after shelf of cheeses, jams, fruit, and meat. They entered and Alistair began a feast.

"Now this is fine dining!" Alistair said as he crunched into a cracker. "Help yourself."

Alistair sat down to fill his stomach with pretzels, cheese, and olives. But Oliver was too nervous to eat.

Then they were spotted by the chef. "You again!" he shouted at Alistair. The chef took a broom and chased the mice out of the pantry. Alistair and Oliver escaped beneath a pastry cart.

"Time for dessert," said Alistair as he feasted on a pie. Oliver was so nervous about the chef that he lost his balance and fell into a cream puff.

When they were finished, the mice went back to Alistair's apartment.

"You take too many risks," said Oliver. "There is a lot of good food here in the city, but I'm too nervous to eat even a crumb!"

"Perhaps you are not cut out for the city, just like I'm not cut out for the country," Alistair said.

The two mice agreed that while they enjoyed visiting one another, each liked his own house and lifestyle better.

Oliver traveled back home and ate a supper of acorns and wheat kernels. Then he curled up under his oak leaves as he listened to the crickets chirp.

Back in the city, Alistair enjoyed the last of his pie and listened to the orchestra play.

Both of the mice sighed, and at the very same time they said, "I love being home."

My Dog Spot

Illustrated by Margie Moore

I have a white dog

Whose name is Spot,

And he's sometimes white

And he's sometimes not.

But whether he's white
Or whether he's not,
There's a patch on his ear
That makes him Spot.
He likes a bone
And he likes a ball,
But he doesn't care
For a cat at all.
He waggles his tail
And he knows what's what,
I'm glad he's my dog,
My dog Spot.

Harmony Farm

Illustrated by Susan Banta

One day on Harmony Farm, Cow looked at Hen curiously. "Hen," she said, "what is it like to lay an egg?"

"It's nice," replied Hen. "The farmer is always happy when he sees a new egg in my roost."

"I thought so," replied Cow. "It looks very exciting. I think I'd like to try it."

All of the animals stopped and stared at Cow.

"Wh-what do you mean, Cow?" asked Cat.

"Don't any of you wonder what it would be like to try something new?" asked Cow.

The animals all confessed that they might like a change. Soon all of the animals traded jobs—all except pig. He was busy eating.

Suddenly Hen cried, "We forgot about Pig!"

The animals walked over to the sty to break the news to Pig. They felt terrible.

"Pig," said Cow, "I'm sorry, but there aren't any new jobs left."

127

Pig let out a sigh of relief. "Thank goodness!" he exclaimed. "I was afraid you were going to ask me to chase mice."

"But Pig," said Hen, "don't you get bored just eating and rolling around in the mud all day?"

"No," replied Pig. "I'm really good at what I do. I can eat slop like nobody's business."

"But wouldn't you like to try something different?" asked Sheepdog. "Like laying an egg?"

"Gosh, no!" replied Pig. "I have a great life."

All the animals set out to do their new jobs—all except pig.

"Cow, what am I doing wrong?" Hen asked, a bit embarrassed that the milk pail was still empty.

"I was wondering the same thing," said Cow. "I haven't laid one egg yet!"

"The sheep just don't respect me," said Donkey.

"How do you pull this plow?" Sheepdog wondered.

"If you think the plow is heavy," said Cat, "try the wagon! Sheesh!"

"And those mice are fast little guys!" chimed in Horse. "I couldn't catch a single one."

Soon all the animals discovered they weren't having much luck with their jobs—all except pig.

Pig watched his friends. They looked so unhappy that he decided to find out what had happened.

Each of the animals told Pig how they had failed at their new jobs.

"Friends," said Pig, "don't think about what you can't do. Think about what you *can* do!" Pig reminded his friends of their unique talents.

The animals felt better and were happy to go back to their old ways. They all felt thankful that they had jobs they could do well. But they were also glad they had tried something new. They were able to laugh about it for years to come.

The Quarrelsome Kittens

Illustrated by Margie Moore

Two little kittens one stormy night,
    They began to quarrel, they began to fight;
One had a mouse and the other had none,
    And that's the way the quarrel begun.

"I'll have that mouse," said the biggest cat.
    "You'll have that mouse? We'll see about that!"
"I *will* have that mouse," said the eldest son.
    "You *shan't* have the mouse," said the little one.

I told you before 'twas a stormy night
    When these two little kittens began to fight;
The old woman seized her sweeping broom,
    And swept the two kittens right out of the room.

The ground was covered with frost and snow,
    And the two little kittens had nowhere to go;
So they laid them down on the mat at the door,
    While the old woman finished sweeping the floor.

Then they crept in, as quiet as mice,
    All wet with snow, and as cold as ice.
For they found it was better, that stormy night,
    To lie down and sleep than to quarrel and fight.

The Lion and the Mouse

Adapted from Aesop's fable
Illustrated by Krista Brauckmann-Towns

One day a lion was taking a nice nap in the warm sun. Nearby, a busy little mouse scurried about looking for berries, but all the berries were too high for her to reach. So she climbed up high and when she reached the very top she discovered that she had accidentally climbed to the top of a lion's head!

The lion did not like to be bothered while sleeping.

"Who dares tickle my head while I'm napping?" the lion roared.

The mouse could see how angry the lion was, so she jumped off his head and started to run away.

But the lion scooped her up in his huge paw. He was furious. "Little mouse," roared the lion, "don't you know that I am the king of the forest? Why did you wake me up from my pleasant nap?"

"Please, lion," pleaded the mouse. "If only you would spare me, I'm sure I will be able to help you in return someday."

The lion roared with laughter.

"How could you, a tiny mouse, help the most powerful animal in the forest?" he chuckled. "That's so funny, I'll let you go—this time."

Then the lion laughed some more as he set her down. The mouse scampered away into the forest.

The lion grew hungry and set out to find lunch.
It wasn't long before he smelled food. As he tracked
the scent, the lion was caught in a hunter's trap!

The lion was stuck under strong ropes, and the
more he struggled, the tighter they held him. Fearing
the hunters would soon return, the lion roared for help.

The mouse heard the lion's roars from far away. At first she was afraid to go back, thinking the lion might hurt her if he saw her. But she remembered the promise she made to help him. She hurried to the lion and found him tangled in the trap.

"Oh, lion," said the mouse, "don't worry! I'll help you get out of there."

"I don't think there's anything you can do," said the lion. "These ropes are very strong. I've pushed and pulled with all my might, but I can't get free."

"I have an idea," the mouse said. "Just hold still, and I'll get to work." She began chewing on the ropes.

She worked and worked, and before long, the mouse had chewed through enough rope for the lion to wiggle his way out of the trap!

The lion was very grateful to the mouse. "Mouse," he said, "thank you for saving me. I'm sorry that I laughed at you when you offered to help me someday."

Then the lion scooped up the mouse, carried her back to the berry bush, and lay down under it.

The mouse climbed onto the lion's back and plucked the biggest berry she could find.

"Let's stick together," she said.

The two have remained best friends ever since.

Little Tommy Tittlemouse

Illustrated by Astrid Kroemer

Little Tommy Tittlemouse
Lived in a little house.
He caught fishes
In other men's ditches.

Little Tommy Tittlemouse
Lived in a bellhouse.
The bellhouse broke;
Tommy Tittlemouse awoke.

Hen and Frog

Illustrated by Michael Hobbs

en and Frog were traveling down the same road. Hen looked up and noticed dark clouds in the sky.

"Oh, dear," clucked Hen. "A storm is coming soon."

"Those clouds are not close," said Frog. "By the time the rain comes we will be home."

Hen knew Frog was wrong.

Hen quickly started to gather straw. "Frog, help me build a house so that we can be safe and dry from the storm," Hen clucked.

"Why?" Frog croaked. "It will only be a few drops."

Hen built a very nice house. It had a window and also a fireplace to keep her warm. Since the storm had not yet come, Hen decided to make a bed.

"Frog, help me make a bed to rest on just in case the storm is a long one," Hen clucked.

"Why?" Frog croaked. "The ground is all that I need to lie on when that little bit of rain comes our way."

Hen knew she would get hungry during the storm.

"Frog, help me gather some mangoes so there will be food when the storm comes," clucked Hen.

"Why?" Frog croaked. "There are many flies to eat."

Hen gathered lots of mangoes and placed them beneath the bed to keep them dry.

Then the storm began. Rain poured down upon the ground, soaking everything.

Frog hopped to Hen's house. "Let me in!" he said.

"No, Frog, you didn't help me build it!" clucked Hen.

"I'll call Cat if you don't let me in," Frog croaked. Hen was very afraid of Cat, so she let Frog inside.

"I'm tired. Let me rest on the bed," croaked Frog.

"No, Frog, you didn't help me build it," clucked Hen.

"I'll call Cat if you don't," Frog croaked.

So Hen let Frog lie on her bed.

"I'm hungry," croaked Frog. "Let me have a mango."

"No, Frog, you didn't help me pick them," said Hen.

"I'll call Cat..." Frog croaked.

"The mangoes are on the roof," Hen fibbed.

Frog hopped to the roof, but there was not a mango in sight. Suddenly, Hawk swooped down and picked Frog up. Hen watched as Hawk flew away with Frog.

When the storm was over, Hen went home and was never bothered by Frog again.

Robin Redbreast

Illustrated by Kathleen O'Malley

Little Robin Redbreast
Sat upon a tree.
Up went Pussycat;
Down went he.

Down came Pussycat;
Away Robin ran.
Says Robin Redbreast,
"Catch me if you can!"

Baby Bluebird

Illustrated by John Kanzler

aby Bluebird looked in the sky. She saw the other birds flying. "I should be flying, too," she said, "but I don't know how."

Her friend Rabbit saw the birds flying, as well, and wanted to help. "Flying looks a lot like hopping," said Rabbit. "If you hop high enough, you might start to fly."

Baby Bluebird decided to try hopping.

She jumped into the air but soon came back down to the ground. Baby Bluebird tried again and again.

"Well," asked Rabbit, "is hopping like flying?"

"It's a little like flying," she said. "But I keep landing. I don't think real flying is so bouncy."

Gopher had been watching Baby Bluebird hopping.

"It seems to me," said Gopher, "that flying is a lot like digging. Maybe if you practice digging with me, it will help you learn to flap your wings and fly."

"I'll give it a try," said Baby Bluebird.

Baby Bluebird found a nice patch of dirt. She flapped her wings, trying to dig a hole.

All her flapping in the dirt did not help Baby Bluebird fly, but she did raise a huge cloud of dust.

"I don't think real flying is this dusty," Baby Bluebird coughed. "I don't know if I'll ever learn to fly."

Turtle heard Baby Bluebird and wanted to help.

"Flying looks a little like swimming," he said. "Maybe if you practice swimming through the water with me, it will help you learn to glide through the air."

So Baby Bluebird dove into the water and tried to paddle alongside Turtle.

"Oh, my! It's so wet!" she cried as she splashed and spluttered. "I don't think real flying is this soggy."

"It's no use," she said. "I might as well stop trying."

"You can't stop trying," said Turtle. "If you want to fly, you must find a way."

Baby Bluebird sat and thought. "Swimming wasn't enough. And neither was hopping or digging," she said. "I think I know what I need to do."

Baby Bluebird took a running start. She hopped like Rabbit. She flapped her wings like Gopher. Once she was in the air, she glided like Turtle and the other birds.

"I'm flying!" Baby Bluebird chirped. She lifted her head and began to sing. It was the happiest song the animals had ever heard.

BINGO

Illustrated by Kat Whelan

There was a farmer had a dog,

And Bingo was his name-o.

B-I-N-G-O, B-I-N-G-O, B-I-N-G-O,

And Bingo was his name-o.

Jackal's Favorite Game

Illustrated by Eric Wilkerson

ackal was a sorry friend. Every day, he'd meet Hare by the lake to play forest games. But being a poor sport and a very selfish creature, Jackal always insisted on having his way. Jackal would tease and tickle Hare until he agreed to play Jackal's favorite game: hide and seek.

That was the way things always were between them.

One day, Hare walked up to Jackal and insisted he would not play if Jackal tickled and teased him.

"All right," Jackal agreed. "But I'll hide first, because I'm bigger than you."

Since this was true, Hare counted. Once he found Jackal, Hare finally got his chance to hide.

As Jackal began to count, Hare bounced off in search of a good hiding place. He went deep into the forest and stumbled upon a small cave. The cave was the perfect spot to hide.

"Okay, here I come," Jackal said as he started the search for his friend.

Jackal looked behind rocks and under bushes.

As Jackal walked deeper into the forest, he finally saw the entrance to the cave. He peeked in. Looking back at him were two enormous green eyes!

"A beast! A beast!" screamed Jackal. Then he ran off as quickly as he could.

"That's not like Jackal," thought Hare. "He loves this game. Why'd he leave so quickly? Who is this beast?"

Hare hopped off after Jackal.

Jackal soon heard the sound of someone running behind him. "Oh, no! The beast is after me!" he cried.

Jackal hid behind a large rock, shaking with fear.

"Please don't hurt me, Beast," Jackal pleaded.

"Oh, Jackal, it's me. Look!" insisted Hare.

Jackal looked up and saw Hare's enormous green eyes. "That was you in the cave?" Jackal asked.

"Yep," said Hare with a laugh.

"Oh, your eyes scared me," Jackal said. "I thought you were a beast! Please don't ever do that again."

"I won't scare you if you promise to be a better friend and not tickle and tease me," replied Hare.

"It's a deal," said Jackal. Then they shook hands and decided to play another game. This time, Hare went first, and he was very happy.

The Kilkenny Cats

There once were two cats of Kilkenny.

Each thought there was one cat too many.

So they fought and they fit,

And they scratched and they bit,

Till, excepting their nails

And the tips of their tails,

Instead of two cats, there weren't any.

The Cat That Walked by Himself

Adapted from the story by Rudyard Kipling
Illustrated by Jon Goodell

ong ago, all of the animals and people lived in the wild nature of the forest. One day Dog, Horse, Cow, and Cat gathered on a hill. They watched Man and Woman build a stone house in the valley below.

"Man and Woman won't be wild for much longer," said Cow.

"I wouldn't give up my freedom to live in a cold stone house," said Cat. "I am a cat, and I walk by myself."

Next the animals watched Man and Woman carry twigs and logs inside. Soon the house glowed with the light of a fire.

"They'll be warm tonight," said Dog. "Warmer than we'll be out here in the forest."

The animals could smell something cooking in the house. "That smells like mutton," said Dog.

So Dog ran down to the house to get a closer sniff. The door to the house opened. Woman came outside and fed Dog a juicy bone.

"I've never eaten a bone so meaty," Dog said to Woman. "I'd give anything to lie by a warm fire and chew bones like this forever!"

"If you hunt with Man and guard our home, we will always give you bones," said Woman.

"Foolish Dog," said Cat. "I would never give up my freedom. I am a cat, and I walk by myself."

Horse, Cow, and Cat saw Dog bound off to help Man hunt every morning and guard the house at night.

They saw Woman playing fetch with Dog. And each night they saw Dog lie by the fire with a juicy bone.

Dog seemed happy to the other animals.

"I'm going to go and visit Dog," Horse said.

Horse trotted down to the house to talk to his friend. When Horse arrived at the house, Woman had just returned from a field with some fresh apples and hay. She gave one of the apples to Horse.

"I've never tasted apples so crisp and fresh. I'd give anything to eat food like this forever," said Horse.

Woman smiled. "You can eat fresh apples all day if you'll help us plant food and carry it home."

Cat hissed at what he saw. "Foolish Horse," he said. "I would never give up my freedom for apples. I am a cat, and I walk by myself."

Cow and Cat watched Horse as he plowed the field and carried the harvest. They saw Man scratch Horse's head, and saw Woman feed Horse every morning.

Cow decided to go talk to her old friends.

Cat watched Cow walk down to the house. Then he saw Woman lead Cow to a patch of grass and clover.

He watched as Cow spent the morning happily munching in the fresh green field.

When Woman came back to get her, Cow said, "I have never tasted grass so fresh or clover so sweet."

Woman smiled. "If you give us warm milk every morning, you may stay in this clover patch forever."

Cat yowled, "Foolish Cow!" He stalked away.

The forest was lonely now. Cat watched Woman milk Cow. He saw Woman stroke Cow's head. Each day Cat smelled fresh milk being carried into the house.

"Perhaps I'll talk to Cow," he said.

Woman saw Cat approach the house. "You can come inside and live," said Woman.

"I'll never give up my freedom," said Cat.

Cat saw a mouse scurry across the floor, and began to chase it. After he captured the mouse, Woman said, "If you stay here and catch mice, there will be milk by the fire every day."

From that day on, Cat lived in the stone house with Dog, Horse, and Cow. Every day, Dog went hunting with Man, Horse plowed the fields, and Cow gave warm milk.

Man and Woman scratched Cat's head and stroked his fur. In return, Cat kept the house free of mice.

Cat spent his days in the house lying by the fire and drinking milk. But at night Cat would disappear to do wild things that only free cats know about. He left when he chose and came back when he wanted.

"I get along quite well with humans, and I like living with them in the house," he said. "But I'm still a cat, and I walk by myself."

Little Kitty

I love little kitty,

Her coat is so warm,

And if I don't tease her,

She'll do me no harm.

So I'll not pull her tail,

Nor drive her away,

But kitty and I

Very gently will play.

Tortoise, Hare, and the Sweet Potatoes

Adapted from the African folktale
Illustrated by Angela Jarecki

As long as anyone remembered, Hare had been a trickster, always up to no good. Hare spent his days telling riddles no one could answer and playing pranks on the animals of the forest.

Tortoise, unlike Hare, was a kind-hearted creature. One morning, Hare stopped by Tortoise's pond to fetch some water.

Tortoise had heard of Hare's bad reputation and thought to herself, "I'll never fall for his trickery."

All afternoon Hare tried his best to trick Tortoise with riddles and pranks. Nothing worked.

Hare thought of a new plan. "Miss Tortoise, please join me for lunch," he said.

"I have no food in my cupboard," said Tortoise.

"No problem," said Hare. "I know of a field full of sweet potatoes ready for harvest. Let's go there."

Tortoise agreed, but with her own plan in mind.

Within minutes, they stepped into a large field and pulled up sweet potatoes until their sack was full.

As Tortoise was about to bite into a fresh sweet potato, Hare said, "Wait! What was that noise?"

Tortoise seemed unconcerned as she bit the potato.

"Shhh! Did you hear that?" said Hare. "We should look around and make sure it's safe! Let's split up."

The two went off in different directions. But Tortoise knew Hare was sneaky. When Hare was out of sight, she crawled into the sack to eat another potato. All of a sudden, potatoes tumbled down all around her.

Hare had picked up the sack, flung it over his shoulder, and sprinted off, hoping to leave Tortoise behind. "She'll never find me," Hare said.

"Boy, will Hare be surprised," Tortoise thought as she ate another sweet potato inside the sack.

After a while, Hare finally stopped running. "Now I can eat all the sweet potatoes, and not worry about Little Miss Slowpoke," he thought. Hare opened the bag.

"Miss Tortoise!" he screamed as she rose from the sack, handing him the last pebble-sized sweet potato.

She grinned and said, "You may be a swindler, but you can't fool me. I'll never fall for your trickery."

Disappointed that his trick backfired, Hare cried and cried. As for Tortoise, she headed back to her pond, happy to have fooled the forest's most famous trickster.

A Fish for You

There once was a fish.

What more could you wish?

He lived in the sea.

Where else would he be?

He was caught on a line.

Whose line if not mine?

So I brought him to you.

What else should I do?

The Fox and the Crow

Adapted from Aesop's fable
Illustrated by Sachiko Yoshikawa

ld Crow was flying high above the treetops one day when he spotted some colorful jelly beans in a jar down below.

"Those sweets look delicious!" said the crow. He swooped down and snatched one up in his beak.

"I sure would like to get that jelly bean," whispered a nearby fox. "I haven't had sweets in a long time. I'll trick the old crow into giving it to me!"

The sly fox slinked over to the tree.

"How handsome you are, Mister Crow," said the fox with a grin.

This got the old crow's attention. He leaned forward to hear the fox better.

"Your feathers are as smooth as a baby fox's fur," said the fox.

The crow leaned closer so he wouldn't miss a single word.

"You're very handsome, indeed," said the fox. "But your voice could cut glass! If it weren't so awful, you could be King of the Birds!"

"What?" hollered the crow.

"My voice is beautiful! Just listen to this:

Caw! Caw!"

As the old crow called down to the fox, the jelly bean fell from his beak. In one quick motion, the fox jumped up and caught the jelly bean. It was gone in a single gulp.

"You're right, Crow," laughed the sly fox. "Your voice is not so bad after all. But your vanity will get you into trouble!"

The Brown Thrush

There's a merry brown thrush

Sitting up in the tree.

She's singing to me! She's singing to me!

And what does she say, little girl, little boy?

"Oh, the world's running over with joy!

Don't you hear? Don't you see?

Hush! Look! In my tree,

I'm as happy as can be!"

Black Beauty

Based on the novel by Anna Sewell
Illustrated by Jon Goodell

he first place that I can remember is a large, pleasant meadow with a clear pond and shady trees. In the daytime I'd run by my mother's side, and at night I'd lie by her to keep warm.

When my mother would go out to work all day, I would stay at home in the meadow with six other colts. I used to run with them and have great fun.

But sometimes our play would get a little rough.

One day, my mother said, "Those colts have not learned their manners. You must be gentle and good, lift your feet when you trot, and never bite or kick."

I have never forgotten my mother's advice.

My master would not sell me until I was four years old. "Boys should not work like men, and colts should not work like horses, until they are grown," he said.

I did learn to go under saddle and in harness. To go under saddle, a horse must learn to wear a saddle and bridle and carry a human on his back. To go in a harness, a horse must learn to pull a cart.

Having to carry a human on my back did feel strange, but I became accustomed to it. And never did I feel more like kicking than when I first wore that harness, but I could not kick such a good master.

In time I got used to everything and could do my work as well as my mother. When the time came, I was sold and left my home for a place called Birtwick Park.

Once in my new stall in the new barn, I met my new neighbors. There was a little pony named Merrylegs and another horse named Ginger. Merrylegs carried the young ladies on her back and took the mistress out in her cart.

My time at Birtwick Park was filled with many adventures. But the incident that stands out most had to do with my mistress.

It was a quiet night when I was awakened by the stable bell ringing loudly. Before I knew it, my groom, John Manly, saddled me and took me at a quick trot to my master's house.

"Now, John," said my master, "you must ride for your mistress's life."

"Yes, sir," replied John, and away we went.

I could tell our ride was important, so I galloped faster than I ever had before.

After an eight-mile run, we came to the doctor's door. John rang the bell and knocked twice. The window flew open. John called to the doctor, "Mrs. Gordon is very ill. She may die if you don't come at once."

The doctor was quickly at the door. "Can I have your horse?" he asked, and John obliged. Soon we arrived home. The doctor went straight into the house and Joe Green, the new stable boy, led me away. My legs shook, sweat covered my body, and I steamed all over.

My mistress never fully recovered from her illness. Soon Ginger and I were sold to a place at Earlshall Park. It was a fine place where we pulled the lady's carriage.

The carriage-pulling would have been a fine post if it were not for the bearing rein. You see, my lady cared what others thought of her, and using the bearing rein on carriage horses was thought to be fashionable.

The bearing rein was a device used to tie a horse's head up to its harness so as to look proud and majestic. But once my head was tied up, I could not put it down. It made my neck sore and breathing difficult.

My career as a carriage horse at Earlshall Park ended when I injured my knees. Reuben Smith, a groom, noticed one of my front shoes was loose. When a boy asked if he should fix it, Smith said no.

Later that night, Smith urged me into a gallop with a sharp cut from his whip. It was very dark, and the roads were stony, but I kept on. Soon the pace and sharp stones took their toll, and my loose shoe flew off. But Smith kept on urging me into a violent pace.

My shoeless foot suffered terribly. Finally I stumbled down on my knees.

I was placed in a livery stable where I was well-fed and well-cleaned. My knees were scarred but my joints were good and I could still work.

There were a good many horses and carriages of different kinds for hire at this livery stable.

Before the livery, I had always been driven by people who knew how to drive. But at this place I would get my experience with all kinds of bad drivers.

As is common in the horse business, I was sold once again. This time I was taken to a horse market. I looked at the young horses and shaggy ponies passing by. I also saw old, broken-down horses that could no longer work.

The man that bought me this time was small, strong, and quick in his motions. I knew in a moment by the way he handled me that he knew horses.

He had a cheery way about him and a kindly look in his eye, too. I knew I would be quite happy with him.

My new master was a cab driver named Jerry Barker. His stables were the old-fashioned kind, but I was kept very clean and given as much food as possible. At night, Jerry would open the door of my stall and let me move about. Best of all, I had Sundays for rest.

When I was put in harness for my cab work, Jerry was very careful to make sure that it fit comfortably. It was as if he were John Manly all over again! And there was no bearing rein. What a blessing!

I never knew a better man than Jerry Barker. He was good and kind, and it was because of him that my long, hard hours of work were tolerable.

Jerry was a good driver, too. He was perfectly trustworthy, even on the busy London streets. And he never laid the whip on me.

Nothing bothered Jerry more than people who were late, wanting a cab horse to be driven hard to make up for their idleness. Jerry would not take these fares.

One holiday season, we had to take two gentlemen to a party at nine o'clock and pick them up at eleven. It was a cold night with a sharp wind and driving sleet.

By the time we got home, Jerry could hardly speak and his cough was dreadful. From what I could understand, poor Jerry was dangerously ill.

Over the next few days, Jerry steadily improved. But I heard his son say, "The doctor said that if Father wishes to become an old man he must never go back to cab work again." It was decided that as soon as Jerry was well enough, the family would move to the country.

I was sold to a corn dealer and baker where Jerry thought I would have good food and fair work. Jerry was right about the good food. But many times, I would have a full load that I had a hard time pulling.

The difficult loads kept on, and soon a younger horse was bought in my place. After being replaced, I was taken to be sold again.

Upon arriving at the market, I found myself in the company of the old broken-down horses I'd seen before. But I felt that any change from my present place would be a great improvement, so I held my head up high and hoped for the best.

Then I noticed a man, a gentleman farmer, with a son and daughter at his side coming from the better part of the market. When he saw me he said, "There's a horse that has known better days."

"Poor old fellow," said the daughter.

"Do you think he was a carriage horse?" asked the son.

233

The man explained that by the look of my ears, shape of my neck, and slope of my shoulder I must have been a very fine carriage horse when I was young.

"Father, couldn't you buy him and make him young again, like you did with Ladybird?" the son begged.

Oh, how I tried to arch my neck, raise my tail, and throw out my legs for them, despite the stiffness.

The man, Mr. Thoroughgood, bought me for five pounds that day.

My new home was a large meadow with a shed.

I was given hay and oats every morning and night, and the run of the meadow during the day.

The boy was proud to have me, and not a day went by that he did not visit. I grew very fond of him.

The perfect rest, good food, soft ground, and gentle exercise were doing wonders for my health. Why, during the winter, my legs improved so much that I began to feel young again.

By the time spring came, my legs were not stiff anymore, and I could pull a cart with perfect ease.

"He's growing young," said Mr. Thoroughgood.

Mr. Thoroughgood added that they must look for a quiet and genteel home where I would be valued.

We came to a white house with a beautiful yard.

A smart young man came out of the house, and as he was looking at my face he said, "That is just like the star that Black Beauty had." In that moment he knew I was Black Beauty, and I knew he was little Joe Green.

I put my nose in his hand to say hello. Never have I seen a man so happy!

I have now lived in this happy place for a whole year. My work is easy and my troubles are over. Joe Green is the kindest of men, and he promised me that I will never be sold again.

Robert Barnes

Robert Barnes, fellow fine,

Can you shoe this horse of mine?

Yes, good sir, that I can,

As well as any other man.

There's a nail, and there's a prod,

And now, good sir, your horse is shod.

The Day Rabbit Came for Pie

Illustrated by Jane Maday

ne rainy afternoon, Kitty decided to make an apple pie. But she would need to pick some apples first.

So she gathered her raincoat, her hat, her umbrella, and her galoshes.

But when Kitty reached the apple tree, she found that the apples were too high.

Bear stopped by.
"If you give me your
hat, I'll pick some apples
for you." Kitty agreed.
But Bear ran off with her hat.
"If I had an umbrella," said Fox,
"I'd help you." But once Kitty handed him
the umbrella, Fox yawned and took a nap.
Wolf walked up. "I'll help, if you
give me your coat. My fur
has been damp all spring."
But Wolf tricked her, too.

Next, Rabbit hopped up to Kitty.

"I'd love to help you out," Rabbit said, "but my feet are too slippery with all this rain. Hey, those galoshes of yours look nice. I bet they would help."

"Take them," Kitty sighed. "They're too big for me."

"Why the long face?" Rabbit asked.

Kitty told Rabbit her sad tale.

"Well, with these galoshes, I can jump to great heights." Rabbit jumped and picked three apples. "You may not have your clothes, but you *will* have pie!"

Rabbit's jumping and talk about pie made the other animals come running.

"Did I hear you say pie?" Fox asked.

Bear saw Fox's umbrella. "My hat is a little small," he said. "Give me that umbrella."

"Where are your manners?" said Wolf. "I'd like the umbrella, please, and a warm piece of pie as well."

The animals began to argue and chase one another around the apple tree.

Bear chased Fox for the umbrella. Wolf chased Bear, shouting about good manners.

The animals ran around and around the apple tree, shedding the hat, coat, and umbrella as they went.

All their running caused the ground to shake—which caused the apples to drop!

While the other animals were distracted, Kitty and Rabbit gathered as many apples as they could possibly carry.

Then the two new
friends fled to Kitty's house.

Kitty took the apples
they gathered and made
delicious pies for them
to share.

"I not only made
pie," said Kitty, "but I
made a friend, too!"

And that was
the day Rabbit
came for pie.

A Dozen Eggs

Illustrated by Margie Moore

I bought a dozen new-laid eggs

From good old Farmer Dickens.

I hobbled home upon two legs

And found them full of chickens.

The Little Red Hen

Adapted from the Russian folktale
Illustrated by Linda Dockey-Graves

There once was a little red hen who had five little chicks. They lived on a farm with their good friends the dog, the cat, and the duck.

One day while sweeping the yard, the little red hen found some wheat kernels. She put them in her pocket and looked for her friends.

250

"Will you help me plant these seeds?" she asked the dog, the cat, and the duck.

The three friends looked at each other. "Heavens, no!" they chuckled.

"Then I'll plant them myself," she said. So the little red hen went to the field and began digging.

Soon her baby chicks came to see what their mother was doing. "Can we help you, Mother?" they asked.

The little red hen was happy that her chicks wanted to help. Together, they planted each seed. They made it a game and the work went quickly.

The dog, the cat, and the duck watched the little red hen and her chicks tend to their plants every day.

One morning, the little red hen found her three friends leaning against the farmer's barn.

"There are weeds in the wheat patch," she said. "Will you help me pull them?"

"I can't," said the cat. "I'll get dirty."

"My leg hurts," said the dog.

"I have to go swimming," said the duck.

"Then I'll do it myself," said the little red hen as she walked to the field with her chicks.

The little red hen knew she must water her wheat so that it would grow tall and strong. She went looking for her friends, who were resting on the porch. The hen said, "Who will help me water my wheat?"

"I'm busy making up a song," growled the dog.

"I'm busy thinking up the words," said the cat.

"I'm busy playing the beat," said the duck.

"I'll just water the wheat myself," said the little red hen. So she and her chicks took the watering can to the garden. The hen pretended to be a thundercloud and sprinkled the chicks with water.

The wheat grew fast. Soon it was fall and the wheat turned golden brown. The little red hen knew it was time to harvest. She found her friends playing cards. The little red hen asked, "Who will help me harvest the wheat?"

The dog, the cat, and the duck kept their eyes on their cards. "Not us!" they said. "We're busy."

"I'll harvest it myself," said the little red hen. So the little red hen and her chicks went into the field to harvest the wheat and tie it into bundles.

"Look at that silly hen," said the dog. "All that work, just to have more work!"

Next it was time for the wheat to be ground into flour. "Who will help me carry the wheat to the miller?" asked the little red hen.

The dog, the cat, and the duck couldn't imagine doing such hard work on such a beautiful fall day.

"Not me," said the dog. "I'm playing a game."

"Not me," said the cat. "I'm playing, too."

"Not me," said the duck. "I'm taking a nap."

The little red hen and her chicks would have to do it themselves. Again, they made a game of the task, and the trip to the miller went very fast.

On the way home, they thought of all the delicious things they could make with their fresh wheat, things like bread, cookies, and cakes.

The next morning the hen and the chicks returned to the mill to pick up their wheat, which had been ground into wonderful, soft flour.

The little red hen called out, "Who will help me bake bread with my flour?"

No one answered her.

"Then I'll bake it myself," said the hen. So she and her chicks mixed and kneaded and baked a loaf of bread.

While the bread baked in the oven, all of the little chicks helped clean up the kitchen.

The smell of baking bread filled the air. The dog, the cat, and the duck peeked into the kitchen.

"Who will eat this bread?" asked the hen.

"We will!" cried the dog, the cat, and the duck.

"You can only have a piece of my bread if you helped me grow it, carry it, or bake it," said the little red hen.

That night, the little red hen and her five chicks filled their tummies with fresh bread.

The dog, the cat, and the duck had none.

Old MacDonald

Illustrated by Daniel Howarth

Old MacDonald had a farm, E-I-E-I-O.

And on this farm he had a cow, E-I-E-I-O.

With a moo-moo here,

And a moo-moo there,

Here a moo, there a moo,

Everywhere a moo-moo.

Old MacDonald had a farm, E-I-E-I-O.

Mimi Moo

Illustrated by Stephen Boulter

imi Moo looked around the farm. All over she saw other animals that looked like they were having fun. Chickens were laying eggs, ducks were swimming, and pigs were rolling around in mud.

She asked her mother if she could go for a walk, and then Mimi Moo headed to the chicken house.

"How do you do? I'm Mimi Moo. May I play with you?" she asked the chickens.

"No, dear, I'm very sorry," said one of the chickens. "We have lots of eggs to hatch."

"I can help!" said Mimi Moo. She climbed up on one of the nests.

"No, no, no!" the chicken clucked. "That just won't do, Mimi Moo!"

Next Mimi Moo decided to visit the duck pond.

She trotted down to the water.

"How do you do? I'm Mimi Moo. May I play with you?" she asked the ducks.

"Jump right in!" said one of the ducks.

Mimi Moo jumped in and created a big wave that splashed the ducks.

"No, no, no!" a duck quacked. "That just won't do, Mimi Moo!"

After that, Mimi Moo decided to visit the pigs.

"How do you do? I'm Mimi Moo. May I play with you?" she asked the pigs.

"If you can fit," said one of the pigs.

Mimi Moo squeezed into the mud.

The pigpen
was awfully crowded.

"No, no, no!" one pig oinked.
"That just won't do, Mimi Moo!"

Mimi Moo decided that it was time to go home.
She trotted back to her field.

When Mama Moo saw her, she said, "Mimi Moo,
what did you do? There's mud all over you!"

Mimi Moo nuzzled her mama. "I tried to be a chicken, a duck, and a pig. I wasn't very good at being any of them."

Mama Moo gave Mimi Moo a lick. "Well, I like you best as a cow," Mama Moo said.

Mimi Moo smiled. "I like that best, too!

The Piper and His Cow

There was a piper had a cow,

Though he had nothing to give her;

Pulled out his pipes and played a tune,

And asked the cow to consider.

The cow considered very well,

And gave the piper some money,

And asked him to play another tune

That she would find quite funny.

Rooster and Fox

Adapted from "The Nun's Priest's Tale" by Geoffrey Chaucer
Illustrated by Elaine Garvin

here once was a farm with very fine chickens. On this farm was a fine, fine rooster who had a fine voice.

He strutted around the barnyard each day, proud of his beautiful crow.

The chickens all agreed that he had the finest voice in the country.

Late one night, when the chickens were roosting in the chicken coop, Rooster awoke with a start. "Hen!" he said. "Hen, wake up. I had a terrible nightmare. I dreamed that a fox crept into the barnyard, looking for the finest, plumpest chicken. And he picked me!"

"It was just a dream," clucked Hen.

"What if it comes true?" asked Rooster. "What if a fox really does creep into the barnyard looking for a fine, plump chicken?"

"Don't be silly," said Hen as she shut her eyes. "Go back to sleep."

Rooster didn't want others to think he was silly, so he didn't tell anyone else about his dream.

A few days later, Rooster was in the barnyard when he saw a fox creeping toward the fence.

"Oh, no!" cried Rooster. "The dream came true. I knew it would. I must run. I must hide."

"My dear Rooster," called Fox. "Don't run away. I didn't come to harm you. I only came here to hear your voice."

Rooster stopped. "My voice?"

"Yes, your voice," said Fox. "Your father had a fine crow. Is your voice as wonderful as his?"

"Of course," said Rooster.

"I'd like to hear it for myself," said Fox.

Rooster puffed his chest, "Cock-a-doodle-doo!"

"Amazing!" said Fox. "Your voice is almost as fine as your father's. Of course, he always crowed with his eyes closed, standing on his tiptoes."

Rooster didn't want to be almost as good as his father. He wanted to crow even better.

Rooster shut his eyes tight and stood on his tiptoes and puffed out his chest.

But just as Rooster opened his beak to crow, Fox grabbed him and leaped over the fence.

"You tricked me!" cried Rooster.

"I flattered you," said Fox. "Flattery always does the trick."

"You're very clever," said Rooster. "And very strong to be able to lift a chicken as plump as me. I wonder if you could lift that rock over there, too."

"Of course," said Fox. He set Rooster down and grabbed the rock. Rooster ran to the barnyard.

"You tricked me!" cried Fox.

"I flattered you," Rooster called out. "Flattery always does the trick!" From then on, he was humble about his voice and kept out of trouble.

Cock-a-Doodle-Doo

Illustrated by Nan Brooks

Cock-a-doodle-doo,
My dame has lost her shoe,
And master's lost his fiddling stick,
Sing doodle-doodle-doo.

The Cock Crows

The cock crows in the morn
To tell us to rise,
And he that lies late
Will never be wise:
For early to bed
And early to rise
Is the way to be healthy
And wealthy and wise.

Androcles and the Lion

Adapted from the ancient folktale
Illustrated by Yuri Salzman

ndrocles was a slave in ancient Rome. His cruel master made him work all day and gave him little food.

One day he decided to run away from his harsh master, even though he knew he would be breaking the law. In the middle of the night he ran deep into the woods.

Androcles sought out a safe place to sleep. Deep in the woods he found a secluded cave that would protect him through the night.

As Androcles slept, a lion was hunting in the woods nearby. The lion was just outside Androcles's cave when he slipped and pierced his paw on a fallen tree branch.

The lion let out an angry roar, which woke Androcles from his deep sleep.

Androcles didn't want the lion to be in pain, so he carefully approached the beast. Though he was scared, Androcles wanted to help the lion.

Androcles was surprised that the huge lion did not charge him or try to harm him.

Gently, he removed the thorn from the lion's paw. After it was gone, the lion rubbed his head against Androcles's shoulder and purred a rumbling purr.

Androcles was no longer afraid of the lion, and the lion was very grateful to Androcles.

From then on, the lion stayed with Androcles. They hunted together and played together. Then one day, a group of Roman soldiers surprised Androcles as he was walking through the woods.

"We are arresting you," said one of the soldiers.

The lion heard the soldiers, but before he could help his friend, they threw a net around him.

It was the custom in ancient Rome for people to watch battles in the great arena. People would come from miles away to see slaves battle lions.

The soldiers forced Androcles to march to the great arena in Rome. "For running away from your master, you will fight a lion!" a soldier said.

On the day of his battle, Androcles gathered his courage as he entered the great arena. Suddenly, a lion burst out of its cage and roared.

295

The lion sprinted toward Androcles, then quickly stopped. Androcles realized the lion in the arena was his good friend from the woods. Androcles embraced his dear friend.

"How did you tame this ferocious lion?" the Emperor asked Androcles.

"I helped him when he needed help," Androcles replied. "That is why he has spared my life."

The Emperor freed them both. The lion went back to the woods and Androcles was a free man in Rome. The two remained friends and never forgot each other.

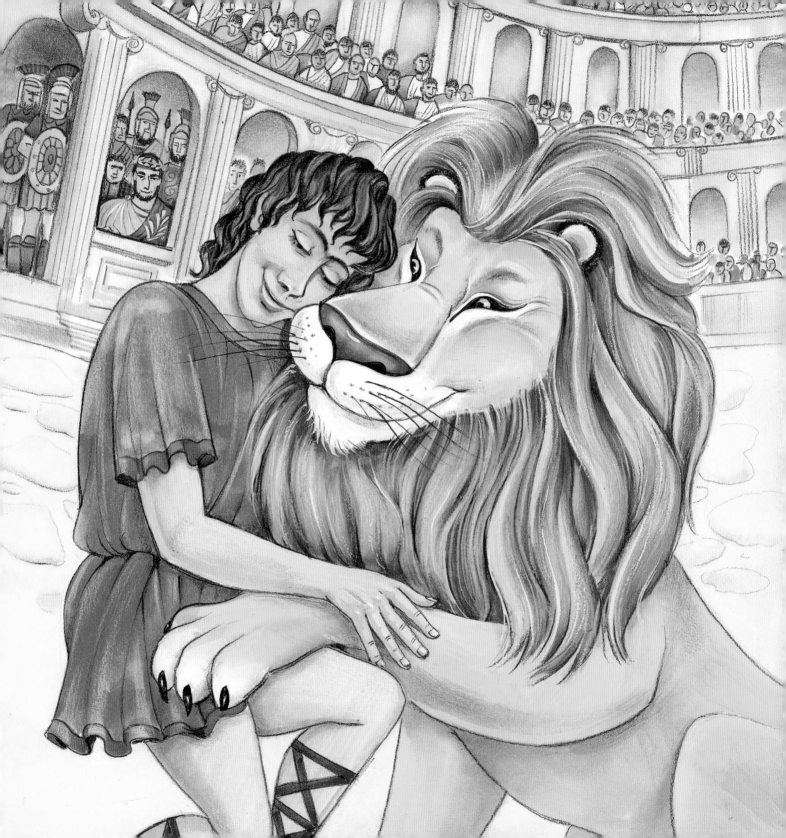

The Canary

Illustrated by Bill Botton

Mary had a little bird,

With feathers bright and yellow,

Slender legs — upon my word,

He was a pretty fellow.

Sweetest notes he always sung,

Which much delighted Mary;

Often when his cage was hung,

She sat to hear Canary.

Bow-Wow

Bow-wow, says the dog;

Meow, meow, says the cat;

Grunt, grunt, goes the hog;

And squeak goes the rat.

Chirp, chirp, says the sparrow;

Caw, caw, says the crow;

Quack, quack, says the duck;

And what cuckoos say, you know.

Brer Rabbit Outfoxes Brer Fox

Adapted from the Southern folktale
Illustrated by Rusty Fletcher

Brer Rabbit was a crafty bunny. He always had a trick up his sleeve.

Brer Fox was tricky, too, and was always trying to catch the rabbit.

Brer Fox knew that Brer Rabbit liked to go to the farmer's garden every day for carrots, so the fox hid by the garden and waited.

When the rabbit came hopping along, Brer Fox jumped out from behind a tree and grabbed him.

"I'm going to brew a stew out of you, rabbit!" said Brer Fox.

"You can cook me in a big pot and serve me for dinner, but please, please don't throw me in that briar patch!" cried Brer Rabbit.

The fox licked his lips. "Maybe that stew would be too much trouble. Maybe I'll roast you instead!"

"You can roast me with potatoes, but please, please don't throw me in that briar patch!" begged Brer Rabbit.

"Seems like the worst thing I could do is throw you in that old briar patch," said Brer Fox. "So that's just what I'll do!"

Brer Fox flung Brer Rabbit into the briar patch. "Oh, no!" cried the little rabbit. But as soon as he landed in the briar patch, Brer Fox heard him giggle.

"You should have known better, Brer Fox!" chuckled Brer Rabbit as he hopped away through the briar patch. "I love this briar patch. It's where I was born. Now you're going to have to find someone else for your dinner!"

Brer Fox was angry, and came up with a new plan. He knew that Brer Rabbit was going to Miss Goose's birthday party. "I'll pretend to be that rabbit's friend and walk him to the party. Then when we cross the river, I'll throw him into the cold water!" Brer Fox said to himself.

The next day, Brer Rabbit was getting ready for Miss Goose's party when he saw Brer Fox on his path. He wrapped himself in a blanket and pretended to be sick.

"What's the matter?" asked Brer Fox.

"I'm sick," sniffed Brer Rabbit.

"Miss Goose is going to be sad if you miss the party. I'll carry you there," offered Brer Fox.

Brer Rabbit thanked the fox for his kindness. The rabbit picked some flowers for Miss Goose and then Brer Fox carried him to the party.

As the fox crossed the bridge, he got ready to throw the rabbit off his back and into the water, but Brer Rabbit was ready for the sneaky trick.

When Brer Fox stopped in the middle of the bridge, the rabbit pulled out a paper bag filled with air and popped it right over the fox's ears.

"Yeeoow!" shrieked Brer Fox as he took off.

Brer Fox thought a hunter was after him and darted across the bridge and down the path.

Everyone at Miss Goose's party could see Brer Rabbit riding Brer Fox down the path.

"That Brer Rabbit is the trickiest critter this side of the Mississippi!" squealed Mr. Pig.

Brer Fox skidded to a stop at the doorstep. "Hello, everyone!" said Brer Rabbit. "Sorry I'm late, but my horse just doesn't run like it used to."

The party guests burst into laughter as poor Brer Fox tried to catch his breath. He had been outfoxed again!

Home on the Range

Illustrated by Jack Hughes

Oh, give me a home where the buffalo roam,

And the deer and the antelope play.

Where seldom is heard a discouraging word,

And the skies are not cloudy all day.

Home, home on the range,

Where the deer and the antelope play.

Where seldom is heard a discouraging word,

And the skies are not cloudy all day.

The Owl and the Pussycat

Written by Edward Lear
Illustrated by Carolyn Croll

The Owl and the Pussycat went to sea

In a beautiful pea-green boat:

They took some honey,

and plenty of money

Wrapped up in a five-pound note.

The Owl looked up to the stars above,

And sang with a small guitar,

"O lovely Pussy, O Pussy, my love,

What a beautiful Pussy you are!"

Pussy said to the Owl, "You elegant fowl,

    How charmingly sweet you sing!"

"Let us be married; too long we have tarried!"

    Said the Owl as he gave her a ring.

They dined on mince and slices of quince,

    Which they ate with a runcible spoon;

And hand in hand, on the edge of the sand,

    They danced by the light of the moon.

The End